City in the
Clouds

A Magical World Awaits You
Read

THE
· SECRETS *·*
- OF -
DROON

THE SECRETS OF DROON

City
in the
Clouds

by Tony Abbott
Illustrated by David Merrell
Cover illustration by Tim Jessell

SCHOLASTIC INC.
New York Toronto London Auckland Sydney
Mexico City New Delhi Hong Kong Buenos Aires

To Debbie O'Hara
with love

Book design by Dawn Adelman

ISBN-13: 978-0-590-10842-3
ISBN-10: 0-590-10842-5

Text copyright © 1999 by Robert T. Abbott.
Illustrations copyright © 1999 by Scholastic Inc.
All rights reserved. Published by Scholastic Inc.
SCHOLASTIC, APPLE PAPERBACKS, and associated logos
are trademarks and/or registered trademarks of Scholastic Inc.

32 31 30 29 28 27 26 25   11 12/0

Printed in the U.S.A.   40
First Scholastic printing, October 1999

Contents

Contents

One

A Spell Returns

School was over for the day.

Eric Hinkle and his two best friends, Neal and Julie, climbed onto the bus home.

"It's been two whole weeks since we've been to you-know-where," Julie whispered as they squeezed into a seat together.

Eric smiled. Of course he knew where.

Droon, the totally secret and magical world of adventure that they had found under his basement.

"It's so strange," Eric said when the bus started up. "We have all these amazing new friends and we can't even talk about them."

"Enemies, too, don't forget," Neal added.

That was true. Since their first adventure in Droon, they had met Galen Longbeard, an old and powerful wizard, and his spidery helper, Max. Khan, king of the pillow-shaped purple Lumpies, had helped them, too.

But their special friend was Princess Keeah, a junior wizard who was trying to keep the wicked Lord Sparr and his red-faced Ninns from taking over her world.

"I wonder what Keeah is up to," Eric said. "I'm itching to go back."

"And I'm just itching!" Neal groaned, bending over suddenly to scratch his legs.

"In fact, I've been doing weird stuff all day. Not to mention the tiny little voices I keep hearing . . ."

That's when it happened.

Pop!

"Whoa!" Eric gasped, looking under the seat. "Look at that!" He pointed at Neal's sneaker.

Neal bent down. His shoelaces stretched and broke, one after another. The toe burst open and something brown and shiny popped out.

"Neal," said Julie, "what's with your sneaker? Is that the stuffing coming out?"

Eric gasped. "No, that's his foot coming out!"

"That's not my foot," said Neal. "It looks like a bug . . . a bug. . . . Wait. That *is* my foot! I've got a bug foot! Oh, no! I'm a bug again!"

The other kids on the bus turned and laughed.

Julie dropped her backpack over Neal's shoe before anyone saw it.

"Holy cow!" Eric whispered. "I know what's going on! Neal, brace yourself. It's back."

Neal frowned. "What's back?"

"The bug spell," he said.

"What?" Neal moaned. "I thought that spell was over!"

"It looks like it just came back," said Julie.

On their last adventure in Droon, a magic spell had gone wrong and accidently Neal had been turned into a bug.

A baby bug, with a hard brown shell, six legs, and feelers on his head that curled and twitched.

And now it was happening again.

Errr! The bus stopped, and the doors swung open.

"There's only one place to go," Eric said, grabbing Neal and pulling him off the bus. "To my basement. Hurry. We need to go back to Droon."

Together, they ran across the yard to Eric's house.

"The spell's not finished somehow," Julie said, frowning. "But don't worry, Neal. Droon is the most magical place ever. We'll find the cure."

"This is *not* going to last forever," Eric added.

"Forever?" Neal squealed. "Yikes!"

They hurried to the side door and opened it. Eric put his finger to his lips. "Nobody can see you like this, Neal." He paused to listen.

Julie nodded. "Let's be as quiet as —"

"A bug?" Neal said. "I can do that."

Eric listened to the clacking of a computer keyboard. "My mom's working." Then he called out. "Mom, I'm home. Neal and Julie are with me. We're going downstairs! Bye!"

They rushed through the kitchen.

On the way, Neal wiped some crumbs off the table, then licked his palm. "Sorry," he said. "Crumbs suddenly seem tasty to me."

Eric was worried. "I don't like this," he said. "Nothing magical has ever happened outside my basement . . . until now."

"Let's think about that *after* Neal's cured," said Julie. She shut the door behind them. They hustled downstairs.

"Now," she said, "did anybody dream of Droon?"

Eric shook his head.

Usually, a dream would call the kids to Droon.

Or the soccer ball in Eric's basement would turn into a globe of Droon. Princess Keeah had put a charm on it.

But the magic soccer ball was lying as usual on the workbench. It was just a ball.

"No dreams," Neal said. "Unless you count the one where I thought a lizard would eat me."

Julie shot Eric a worried look. "That's good enough. Come on."

They went to a door under the basement stairs.

Eric quickly opened the door and turned on the light. Everyone piled into a small room. He closed the door behind them.

"Ready?" he asked.

Neal held up his right hand. His fingers had started to form a claw. "I don't know about you, but I am!"

Julie flicked off the light.

Whoosh! The floor vanished instantly and the magic stairs appeared. Without wasting another moment, Eric darted down the steps.

Each time he and his friends had gone to Droon, the stairs had taken them somewhere different. He wondered where the stairs would lead this time.

"I see clouds!" Julie said. "We're in the air!"

Rrrr. A rumbling sound came from the clouds.

"Sounds like something is coming," Neal said.

Suddenly, the clouds parted. A round silver shape passed slowly under the bottom step.

"Whoa! It's some kind of huge flying thing," Julie said. The rainbow-colored stairs began to ripple under them.

"As usual, the stairway is fading too soon," Eric said. "We'd better jump." Then he gripped his friends' hands firmly.

Together, they jumped.

Plink! Plonk! Plunk! They landed on the ship.

"There's a hatch over there!" Julie shouted.

Freezing wind blew over them as they crawled across the silver surface to a small door.

Eric tried to open the hatch. "It's locked!"

Neal leaned over. He gripped a corner of the hatch with his clawed hand and twisted.

Krrnch! The little door sprang open to reveal a metal ladder running down inside the ship.

"At least being a bug makes me strong!" Neal said. "Let's go!"

One by one, the three friends went down into the strange flying ship.

Two

The Silver Ship

Eric reached up, grabbed the twisted hatch, and pulled it down over them. "Okay, we're on a flying ship. But whose flying ship? And where is it going?"

They looked around. They were in a narrow corridor. The walls were made of the same shiny metal as the outside of the ship.

"My bug senses are returning," said Neal. Then he pointed ahead of them.

"I hear voices this way. But I can't tell who."

"Let's find out," said Julie.

Carefully, they crept along the corridor. Neal's bug foot clomped on the floor. Eric followed behind.

They rounded a corner in the narrow hall.

Julie stopped. "Uh-oh . . ."

Hanging on the wall ahead of them was a row of shiny black armor, glinting in the light.

"That's Ninn armor!" Eric said. "There are Ninns on board! Maybe even Lord Sparr!"

"We're in enemy territory, folks," Neal added.

The ship rumbled noisily around them. It seemed to be changing direction.

The three friends quietly inched their

way to a large metal door with a wheel on it.

"A Ninn-sized hatch," Eric whispered. "Here goes nothing." He turned the wheel and opened the hatch slightly.

They peered into a large circular cabin filled with Ninn warriors. The Ninns were working the giant ship's controls.

Eric shivered. His friends huddled closer.

One Ninn stepped over to a red chair. The kids couldn't see who was in the chair.

"King Zello and his daughter are heading for the city of Ro, my lord," the Ninn grunted. "What shall we do?"

"Set course for the valley!" snarled a familiar voice.

"It's Lord Sparr!" Eric whispered.

"Soon we shall have the magic diamonds — millions of them," the Ninn grunted happily.

"The diamonds will be useful," Sparr said. "But what I really seek in the city of Ro is a single word. . . ."

Eric frowned. *A word? What word?*

The pink clouds thinned as the giant ship began to slip down through them. The cabin windshield showed a world of white mountains. Here and there were slithering silver rivers. A broad, flat valley directly ahead was circled by forests of violet and blue trees.

The world of Droon.

Pop! Neal's other sneaker began to split.

"Oh, man!" Neal moaned loudly. Too loudly.

Sparr bolted up from his throne and turned around. His dark eyes flashed when he saw the children. "Spies! Seize them!"

Instantly, three large Ninns rushed over and grabbed the children.

The red guards' grips were like steel.

"Let us go, Sparr!" Julie exclaimed.

Sparr laughed. "That's exactly what I intend to do! Ninns, take them to the platform!"

The sorcerer's bald head gleamed as if it had been polished. And small dark fins grew behind each ear.

"Do you expect us to talk?" Eric asked.

"No, I expect you to . . . fly!" Sparr replied.

Without another word, the big red warriors hustled them roughly into the corridor.

"Where are you taking us?" Neal asked.

"You'll find out!" one Ninn laughed. He pressed a button on the corridor wall and — *whoosh!* — a door in the side of the ship opened.

The children found themselves on a small metal plank jutting out from the ship.

The wind howled around them.

"Okay," said Eric, "I'm guessing that this platform is not a good thing."

"We call it the tossing platform!" one of the guards said with a grunting sort of laugh. His black eyes seemed like tiny marbles in his puffy red face.

"We toss, you fly!" another Ninn said.

"And what if we can't fly?" Julie asked.

"Splat!" The third Ninn laughed.

The kids all looked at one another.

"Okay, now I'm worried," Neal said.

"And you weren't up till now?" Julie cried.

Suddenly — *zzzzzz-blam!* — the ship rocked.

Ka-blam! Boom! The sky lit up with sparkling blue beams. Dozens of plump purple ships swooped out of the clouds.

The ships were small and round and very fast. Two wings stuck out on each side of a clear bubble.

"The Lumpies!" Julie shouted.

The Ninns grunted and ran inside. The iron door closed behind them. The kids were trapped outside the ship.

"Now I'm really worried!" Neal said. "We really *are* going to go splat!"

Suddenly, one of the purple planes swept underneath the platform. It pulled up sharply. Its cockpit bubble opened. There were two figures inside. "Jump! Quickly!" yelled the pilot.

They did. "Oomph! — whoa! — yeow!"

The ship circled up and away into the pink clouds as the kids tumbled onto soft purple pillows. They landed right next to a small purple creature who looked like a chubby pillow himself.

The creature's cheeks bulged like bubblegum bubbles.

"Khan!" Eric cried.

"King of the Lumpies, at your service!"

Khan said, his short arms flying over the controls.

Zzzz — blam! The back end of the little ship roared with the sound of blasting. A helmeted creature behind them leaned over a strange gun.

Sparkling blue beams of light burst on the giant silver ship below. Sparr's airship changed direction and veered away.

"Lumpies one, Sparr zero!" Khan cheered.

"Nice blasting from your helper back there," Julie said to Khan. "Amazing, whoever that is!"

"She ought to be," Khan said with a twinkle in his eye. "That's Princess Keeah!"

Three

The Flying City of Ro

Princess Keeah tore off her helmet. Her long blond hair tumbled to her shoulders. "I'm so glad to see you!" she said. "We were on our way to meet my father when Sparr attacked us. But why are you here?"

Neal held up his claw. "The spell from last time sort of . . . came back."

"Oh, my!" the princess gasped.

"Plus," Eric added, "then we heard that

Sparr plans to steal diamonds from a place called Ro!"

Keeah glanced at the Lumpy leader.

"We have no time to waste," Khan muttered. He pulled on the lever and they soared up into the pink clouds.

"What's going on?" Julie asked.

Keeah turned to her friends. "My father and I were supposed to meet Galen and Max at the city of Ro to find out where my mother is."

Eric nodded. On one of their previous journeys, they had learned that Keeah's mother, Queen Relna, was not dead as everyone had thought. A witch had told them she was alive.

"Where is this city of Ro?" Julie asked.

"Everywhere!" Keeah answered. "Ro is a flying city. It flies constantly over all of Droon."

"Cool!" Neal said, scratching his neck.

"Very cool, as you say," Khan said. "And on any other day Sparr would not be able to attack it."

"Why is today so important?" Eric asked.

Khan pulled the purple ship higher. "Ro hides itself under a spell of invisibility."

"Except," said Keeah, "that one day each year Ro becomes visible. It lands in the Kalahar Valley to collect diamonds. The magic jewels hold the power of invisibility."

"Those are the diamonds Sparr is after," Julie said.

Eric was drawn to the small ship's front windscreen, where a large white bird soared along with the purple ship.

"The white falcon!" he said. He remembered all the times he'd seen it before in Droon.

Keeah smiled. "The falcon is always nearby, watching over what we do." Then she turned.

"Neal, I'm sorry the spell came back," she said. "But you're in luck. The Guardians live in Ro. They are very old and very wise. They know more than anyone about, well, anything! They can help you."

Khan sniffed. "But we must hurry. At midnight, Ro vanishes again. Once it does, it will be impossible to leave for a whole year!"

The small winged craft shot over a range of snowy mountains and dipped to a desert plain.

A few moments later, Khan landed on the outside of a ring of tall hills.

"The Kalahar Valley is beyond these hills," Keeah said, stepping from the ship. "Come."

As the sun lowered into afternoon, the

small band crept through a narrow pass in the hills.

"Oh, my gosh!" Julie exclaimed as they tramped out to a ledge on the other side.

The valley below teemed with hundreds of Ninn warriors. They were armed with bows and arrows and swords. With them were dozens of winged lizards called groggles.

Suddenly, a great cry rose up from the red warriors. They looked skyward to see Sparr's silver airship circling the valley.

But that was nothing compared to what happened next.

On the far side of the valley, the drifting pink clouds slowly parted.

Over the hills came a giant city. It looked as if it had been uprooted from the earth. Slowly, it floated downward into the center of the valley.

"Ro!" Keeah whispered excitedly. "I hope my father made it there safely. And Galen and Max, too."

"It's awesome," Eric exclaimed, looking up.

The city was built on an enormous floating disk that seemed to stretch for miles across.

Strangely shaped towers spiraled to the sky. Bridges soared from one side of the city to the other. Domes of green, pink, and blue topped buildings of every shape and size.

And the lights! The whole city gleamed and sparkled as if every inch of it were lit!

"Ro is a city of peace, ruled over by the wisest of people, the Guardians," Khan said.

"But now Sparr is waiting for it," Keeah said with a shiver.

The city finally rumbled to the ground, nestling into the valley as if it had always been there.

As soon as it landed, a white ray of light shot from the city to the valley floor.

"They are drilling for the diamonds," Khan whispered.

A moment later, millions of tiny glittering rocks flowed back through the light to the city.

"They're drilling with light," said Neal.

"How can we get in?" Eric asked. "There's an army of Ninns between us and the city."

The Lumpy king sniffed suddenly. The kids remembered that Lumpies were expert sniffers.

"We're in luck," the purple king said. "I smell a flock of wild groggles roosting nearby. And the Ninns don't know about them."

"Groggles?" Neal muttered. "Those flying lizards *eat* bugs like me. Anyone have a Plan B?"

"But Khan's a groggle whisperer!" Keeah said.

"A what?" asked Eric.

"I talk softly to them," Khan said with a chuckle. "And the groggles listen. The wild ones who live in the mountains are actually quite nice."

The five friends crept slowly up to a flock of groggles nesting on the edge of the valley.

In the sky above, Sparr's silver airship circled the giant city and swooped down into it. As if this were a signal, the Ninns jumped onto their own groggles. A moment later, Sparr's flying army swarmed up from the valley floor.

"Quickly now!" Keeah cried. "Ro will soon take flight."

"Psss!" Khan whispered soft words into one lizard's ear. It grunted, dipped for everyone to climb on its back, then lifted from the ground with a great flapping of wings.

With the kids clutching the groggle tightly, it soared up to join the others.

Four

Into the Palace

"Psss-psss-psss!" Khan whispered. The groggle obeyed, circling high over the city.

"There it is!" Keeah exclaimed. "The Guardians' palace has the tallest tower."

Below them stood a palace of shiny gray stone. From its top a tower coiled up to the sky. It was the tallest and strangest of all the buildings in the city.

The groggle landed clumsily on a small

street near the palace and the kids piled off. The streets were deserted.

"The people of Ro are peaceful," Khan said. "They will likely be hiding."

"First things first," said Eric. "We need to find a cure for Neal."

"No," said Neal. "First we stop Sparr."

"Finding the Guardians will help us do both," said Keeah.

Julie pointed into the air. "We'd better find them soon. Here comes Sparr's silver ship."

They watched from the corner as Lord Sparr's airship landed in a large square in front of the palace. Almost immediately, a hatch opened and Lord Sparr himself appeared.

"Princess Keeah," Khan whispered, "I will try to find your father and tell him where we are. With my nose, I should be able to sniff myself past Sparr and his chubby guards."

The kids wished the Lumpy king good luck.

Suddenly, the street beneath them rumbled. The stones vibrated under their feet.

"We're flying!" Neal said. "Ro is going up!"

They peered between the buildings to see the foothills slip away below them. The air grew colder. Clouds drifted over the rooftops. Ro was in the air once again.

"Let's roll!" Julie cried. "Before it's too late!"

The band of friends crept into the first hallway they could find. It was dark and cool.

"Okay," said Eric. "Where should we go?"

Keeah pointed into the darkness. "My

father says, when in doubt, head for the center."

"Looks kind of spooky in there," Julie said.

"I like the dark," said Neal. "I can actually see better. I hear voices, too. Not Ninns, though. I think this is the way."

They followed Neal deeper into the palace.

Julie turned to Keeah. "Why does Ro become invisible?"

"To protect the Tower of Memory," the princess answered. "Everything that happens in Droon is written in the Tower. The Guardians are keepers of the Tower and of the whole history of our world. My father and I hoped they might tell us what happened to my mother."

"Do you think they can help debug me?" Neal asked.

Keeah nodded. "That's my plan."

"Cool," said Neal. "Then that's my plan, too!"

Together, the four friends scurried up a set of steps to another level. They could still feel the city rising higher and higher into the air.

Strange noises echoed behind them.

Eric wondered if the Ninns were on their trail. Did Sparr already know they were there? And if he found them, what would he do? *Splat?*

"The Guardians rule over the people of Ro," Keeah added. "They're the last of a band of knights who have lived since the earliest days of Droon."

Suddenly, Neal stopped short and everyone bunched up behind him.

"What's the matter?" Eric asked.

"The hall ends here," his friend said.

"Well, that's dumb," said Julie. "Why would they have a hall that leads nowhere?"

Keeah chuckled. "The hall may end, but the way continues." In the dim light, she pointed to a strange mark on the wall above them.

"What is it?" Julie asked.

"It's an ancient language," Keeah said, peering close. "I don't know all the words, but I know this one. It means . . . the Guardians!"

Keeah pushed at the wall.

Vrrrt! It slid aside easily.

The children slipped through the opening.

They found themselves in a tall room with a curved ceiling.

"I should tell you one more thing about the Guardians," Keeah said. "They are —"

"Oh, my gosh!" Julie gasped.

"Whoa!" Eric grunted.

"I think we found where they keep the dinosaurs!" Neal whispered.

Five

The Guardians of Droon

In the center of the room were two seven-foot-tall lizards with large heads. They stood upright, swishing their heavy tails across the tiled floor.

Their short upper arms ended in six-inch-long clawed fingers. Their teeth were even longer.

But the strangest part was that they were dressed in shiny green robes.

"Let's . . . um . . . sneak back out," Eric said.

"Before they see us . . ." Julie added.

But Keeah walked slowly up to the creatures.

"Ah!" said one of the dinosaurs. "Princess Keeah and her friends from the Upper World!"

"Welcome to the city of Ro," the other said.

Eric blinked. "Are you . . . dinosaurs?"

"Theropods, actually," one said. "I'm Bodo."

"And I'm Vasa," said the other. "We're the Guardians!"

Bodo pulled a pair of spectacles from his robe and slipped them on. He stepped over to Neal. "You must be Neal, the boy with the problem."

Neal blinked. "How did you know my name?"

The creature smiled. "I was reading in the Tower this morning. I knew you were coming."

"Then you know that Sparr is here, too?" Keeah said. "And his Ninns are everywhere."

Vasa hissed between his teeth. "Sparr has come for the diamonds. He wants to harness their power for his own evil ends."

"Then we must hurry," Bodo said.

Vasa put a claw to his chin and walked around Neal. "Hmm. Yes, I see. We must find out exactly what happened the instant you became a bug. You must read what Quill has written about it in the Tower of Memory."

"Who is Quill?" Eric asked.

"Our magic feather," Vasa said. "All of Droon's history — all that has ever happened — Quill writes in the ancient language. He writes everything on the stones of the Tower."

"And sometimes," Bodo said with a chuckle, "Quill writes so fast, he gets ahead of himself."

Keeah frowned. "What do you mean?"

It was Vasa's turn to laugh. "He means that Quill writes what hasn't happened yet!"

"You mean . . . the future?" Eric asked.

"Oh, yes," Bodo replied. "But what we need now is from the past." He scribbled on a small square of paper and handed it to Neal.

On the paper was a strange drawing.

"What's this?" Neal asked.

"Your name, in the ancient language," Bodo replied. "And here are the rest of your names."

Eric   Julie   Keeah

The children took the papers from Bodo. He also gave them small writing tools that looked like pencils.

Vasa stepped over to Keeah. "But you, Princess, you are here for something else?"

She nodded. "My father and I were coming to see what you could tell us about where my mother is. We know she is alive . . . somewhere."

Vasa nodded slowly. "Queen Relna was — is — a great ruler, as is your father, King Zello."

Keeah breathed deeply and continued. "She fought Lord Sparr at the forbidden city of Plud. She was never seen again."

"Princess, you must look for this symbol."

"Your mother's name. Relna. Also this one."

"Who is that?" Julie asked.

"Lord Sparr," Eric said, though he wasn't sure why. "Am I right?"

Bodo and Vasa shared a look at each other, then nodded. "Indeed, you are correct, Eric."

Clang! Boom! Blam!

Bodo raised his claw. "Sparr has entered the palace! Go to the Tower quickly. Take these symbols. Read the characters next to them and bring back what you have found out. All your questions will be answered."

"But what about you?" Keeah asked.

"Sparr will not harm us today," Vasa said.

Clomp! Clomp!

"Ninns!" Neal hissed. "We're too late!"

"A simple spell will help you escape capture," Vasa said. He took a book from a nearby shelf and held it open. "Keeah, say these words."

Bodo nodded to Keeah. "Only a true wizard, even a young one, can perform spells. Hurry!"

Keeah began to read. "Bello . . . gum . . ."

Clomp! Ninn footsteps echoed just outside.

"Pello . . . mum . . ."

"What's going to happen?" Julie asked.

"Rello . . . hum!"

Fwoot — boomf — pahhh! The room filled with thick blue smoke just as the doors blasted open.

Light from a dozen blazing torches filled the small room. Ninn warriors entered and grabbed Bodo and Vasa roughly.

Then the doorway filled with a dark shape. Lord Sparr entered.

Eric expected the sorcerer to start screaming.

He'd toss the kids off the flying city. *Splat!*

Sparr strode over to Eric and his friends.

"My noble warriors," Sparr boomed. "How does the battle go?"

Eric blinked. He gasped. Then he looked over at Neal and Julie. He nearly choked when he saw their faces. They were thick and red. Their cheeks were all puffy. They growled with angry looks. Then he looked down at himself.

"Ungh!" he grunted.

Eric and his friends were . . . Ninns!

Six

Working for Lord Sparr

Eric tugged at the skin on his arm. It was rough and thick and oily. "Yuck," he muttered.

Neal, Julie, and Keeah pinched their skin, too.

"I'd rather be a bug!" Neal whispered.

"King Zello and the Lumpies have landed," Sparr said. "How is our attack going?"

"Um . . . really good," Neal said with a grunt.

"Good?" Sparr repeated.

"Lots of Lumpies ran away."

"And . . ." Sparr said.

"King Zello has fallen back," Keeah said, groaning in a deep voice as a Ninn might do.

"And the wizard, what's his name?" Julie boomed.

"Galen," Sparr said with a snarl.

Eric snorted. "Don't expect to see him for a while!"

Sparr smiled evilly. "You have done well. Go gather diamonds with the others." Then he turned to Bodo and Vasa.

Vasa hissed as Sparr approached. "You won't get away with this, Sparr . . ."

"Ah, yes, the Guardians," Sparr scoffed. "Last of the peace-loving knights of Droon's distant past. You are no threat to me, you . . . fossils!"

Bodo narrowed his lizardy eyes at the sorcerer. "Beneath the cloak of invisibility, Ro has prospered for centuries. Beneath the cloak of peace lies great power."

Lord Sparr's face went pale. "We shall see how powerful you are when I use your diamonds to create an invisible army!"

Then he snapped his fingers.

Another troop of Ninns wheeled in a long wooden cart brimming with the most dazzling white jewels Eric had ever seen.

Magic diamonds.

"Have you found them all?" Sparr growled.

The Ninn bowed his head. "Not all, my lord."

Eric looked at his own hands again. They were big and red and puffy, with six fingers. He started to feel sick. A wave of

dizziness came over him. He felt hot and cold at the same time.

His stomach rumbled.

Then he felt himself shrinking inside his Ninn armor. He was changing back!

He looked over at Julie, Neal, and Keeah. They, too, were beginning to change. In a moment, they wouldn't be Ninns anymore!

Eric grunted. Even his voice was changing.

Sparr flashed a look at him. "What is it?"

"We . . . um . . . better check on our groggles," he said, hoisting up his leather pants, which were beginning to slip down on him. "Gotta give them biscuits or they get mad."

Sparr squinted. "Biscuits?"

"Um, right!" Keeah blurted out, her

voice not so deep anymore. "Then we'll go find those pesky kids. And that princess. You know, the junior wizard. She's powerful, but we can take her."

Eric's eyes gaped. He nudged Neal. Neal's foot was turning back into a bug foot.

"If you find the children, throw them off the side!" Sparr boomed. "Go! We leave Ro soon!"

Neal grabbed Eric, Julie, and Keeah. They clomped out the door and ran until they were out of breath.

"Bodo and Vasa could have told us we were on a timer!" Eric exclaimed when they were far away from the Guardians' room.

Julie bit her lip. "We need to split up. You guys head to the Tower and find Neal's cure. I'll see if I can help Bodo and

Vasa. We'll meet at the front steps in an hour."

"Half an hour," Keeah said. "Ro will disappear very soon. Look."

They all looked out a window in the hall. Outside the palace, the sky was turning a deep blue. The moon shone through puffy white clouds.

"It's nearly midnight," Keeah said. "We haven't much time."

"I'll go with Julie," Neal said. "My bug sense may help us stay away from Ninns. Real Ninns."

"Neal, you'll be normal again soon," Eric said, patting his friend on the back. Then he stopped. Neal's back was as hard as a shell.

Eric swallowed hard.

Neal was getting worse. Much worse.

"Come on, Keeah," Eric said. "To the Tower!"

The gang split up. With Ninn footsteps echoing all around them, Eric and Keeah threaded their way toward the center of the palace.

To the giant Tower of Memory.

Seven

Written in Stone

The Tower of Memory was a huge spiral of stones coiling up from the ground.

Eric and Keeah entered a vast inner courtyard, looked up, and saw it.

"It's huge," Eric whispered.

Row upon row of rough gray blocks circled higher and higher into the starlit sky.

"Do you have the papers with our

name symbols?" Keeah said, spotting a narrow opening in the tower.

"Yes." Eric clutched Neal's square of paper, along with his own and Julie's. "Let's do it."

They slipped through the opening.

The inside of the tower was empty and very quiet. The only noise was a faint scratching sound from above.

Eric squinted up. There, on the very top row of stones, barely visible in the mist and moonlight, was the magic feather, Quill. It scratched word after word into the stones, writing quickly, then stopping, then writing faster than ever.

Whenever it filled one stone with the strange words and symbols, another stone mysteriously appeared next to it. Quill filled that one and went on to another. And another.

"This is so weird," Eric said softly. "The

Tower is building itself. It keeps getting taller."

"Quill writes what happens to everyone," Keeah said. "Everything that has ever happened in Droon is right here."

"And some things that haven't happened yet."

Eric turned a complete circle as he followed the rows of silvery gray stones, looking for the strange symbols the Guardians had given them.

Keeah breathed out suddenly.

"What?" Eric said, turning to her.

"My mother's symbol!" she said, running to the wall nearest her. "And Sparr's! I see them. That must be it! What happened to her at Plud!"

She began scratching down the strange words with the pencil Bodo had given her.

Then Eric saw his own name among the carvings. "Oh, wow!"

Next to it were Julie's and Neal's names. He scanned the lower rows to see if the names appeared before then. No, they didn't. But their names were written many times after that. He looked up as far as he could. Their names were still there, curving into the upper rows.

All the way into the future?

Would he and his friends do many things in Droon? Eric wished he could read the top row, to find out what the future might bring. He, too, started scribbling down the strange words for the Guardians to decipher.

Keeah uttered something softly. Eric turned to see her slip quietly out of the Tower.

He was about to call out to her, then

stopped. The hair on the back of his neck stiffened. He knew someone else was in the Tower with him.

Slowly, Eric turned his head. There, standing in the exact center of the room, was a tall, dark figure. A man.

Eric gasped to himself.

The man was Lord Sparr.

Sparr stood motionless, reading the walls of the Tower and mumbling the words to himself. As he did, tears welled in his eyes, glinting in the moonlight from the Tower's top opening.

One tear trickled down Sparr's cheek. He flicked it away instantly. The teardrop hit the stone floor, hissing on the cold stones. *Ssss!*

"Oh, whoa!" Eric breathed.

Suddenly Quill began scratching on the stones more speedily than before. Eric remembered what the Guardians had said.

Sometimes Quill writes so fast, he writes what hasn't happened yet.

Sparr raised his eyes toward a single spot on the upper walls.

As Eric watched, the sorcerer lifted off the ground and flew up to the top of the Tower.

Quill kept scratching faster and faster. He filled one stone after another.

Eric knew. Quill was writing the future.

An instant later, Sparr was back.

Eric could not move, could not breathe. It seemed like hours that Sparr just stood there.

Then, a strange sound came from the sorcerer. A sound like all his breath leaving him.

And out of that breath came a single word.

"Ice."

Sparr began to laugh softly.

Eric felt as if he would explode. He needed to sneeze. Then cough. He felt as if he couldn't hide a second longer. And yet he had to be quiet. Or Sparr would see him and hurt him. *Splat!*

Just then, a white shaft of moonlight suddenly fell into the Tower from the opening above. Eric pressed himself back against the stones, but the shaft of light moved across the floor to him.

Sparr turned instantly. His eyes flashed red.

He saw Eric. He stared right at him!

Clomp! Clomp! A troop of Ninns tramped into the tower. "It is time, Lord Sparr," one said.

The moonlight dimmed behind a cloud and Eric was in shadow once more.

Sparr nodded. "I have seen what I came here for."

Sparr was still staring at Eric. He could destroy Eric in a second!

Then why?

Why?

Why did Sparr simply wrap his long black cloak around him and walk out of the Tower?

Eight

Neal and Company

Clomp! Clomp! The Ninns tramped through the halls and out of the palace.

Sparr went with them.

"Eric!" Keeah ran back into the tower. "I was so scared when you didn't follow me."

Eric nodded slowly. "I couldn't move," he said. "Sparr saw me, but . . . he let me go."

Keeah's eyes widened. "Eric, we need

to get back to the Guardians. Ro will disappear soon, and we'll disappear with it."

They rushed back to the Guardians' room. The Ninns had gone. Vasa and Bodo were free.

"Neal and Julie have gone to see where Sparr is taking the diamonds," Vasa said quickly. "What did you find in the Tower?"

Trembling, Keeah handed her paper to them.

"Ah, the secrets of Droon's past," Bodo said.

Vasa peered over his shoulder and began to translate what Keeah had written. "At the city of Plud, Lord Sparr nearly killed Queen Relna."

"But, you see," Bodo went on, "the witch Demither put a curse on Relna. Instead of suffering death, the queen assumed an animal form."

Keeah gasped. "An animal? Is it . . ."

"Yes," Bodo said, squinting at the words. "A white bird. A falcon."

"I knew it!" Keeah cried, jumping for joy. "That's why the falcon is always there! It's my mother following me, watching over us!"

"But Demither told us the queen was in prison," Eric said.

"True," Vasa went on. "Such a curse is a kind of prison. But now the queen needs your help if she is ever to be human again. Hers is a dangerous journey, filled with many trials."

Keeah wiped away a tear. "I will help her."

"So will we," said Eric, smiling at the princess.

Vasa turned to Eric, "And what did you discover?"

Eric gulped as he handed the paper to Vasa. "Sparr saw me, but he just . . . walked away."

Bodo glanced at Vasa, then peered through his spectacles at Eric. "And you have a question."

Eric nodded. "Does what Quill writes *have* to happen? I mean, can the future be *changed*?"

"We won't know that until the future becomes the present," said Bodo.

Eric frowned. "But . . ."

Suddenly, Julie and Neal rushed into the chamber.

"The diamonds are being loaded into Sparr's airship!" Julie said breathlessly. "He looks like he's leaving the city."

"And look at me," Neal said. "I'm getting way worse!" He held up his hands. They were both claws now.

"Quickly, Neal, stand here," said Vasa,

holding Eric's writing up to the light. Together with Keeah, the Guardians began
to mumble strange words. "Timbo . . .
limbo . . . koo-kimbo!"

Poomff! A huge ball of smoke appeared
in the chamber. A moment later, Neal
walked out.

He looked normal. He held up two normal hands. His sneakers were still ripped,
but human toes were sticking out. He
broke into a smile.

"Yes!" he cried. "I am back!"

"Me, too!" cried another voice.

Everyone turned to see a second Neal
emerge from the smoke.

"Uh-oh," said Keeah.

Two Neals walked around the room.
Twins!

"Ah, yes," Vasa said. "This is a normal
side effect of the spell. Only temporary.
Don't worry."

The first Neal smiled. "I always thought two Neals were better than one!"

"Slap me five, brother!" said the second.

Rrrrr! The walls began to shake.

"Ro is turning invisible again," Bodo said. "Go. This way is quickest!" He pointed to a secret door in the chamber.

"It leads to the square outside," Vasa added. "Good luck to you all! May you find your mother, Princess. And farewell to you, Neal."

"Thanks!" said Neal.

"Same here!" said the other.

Eric, Keeah, Julie, and the two Neals rushed through the door and outside the palace.

Clomp! Clomp! The square was crawling with Ninns. They were loading the diamonds into the cargo area of Sparr's silver ship.

"We've got to get those back!" Keeah said.

"And I've got to find out why Sparr let me go," Eric whispered.

"Does anybody have a plan?" Julie asked.

"I've got a plan!" boomed a strange, loud voice from the shadows nearby. "How about we form a human wall and blast our way in!"

"Wh-wh-who is that?" Keeah whispered.

The shadows stirred and out stepped a large man with bright green armor. He had a helmet with horns on it. He carried two wooden clubs.

"Whoa!" one Neal mumbled.

"A Viking!" said the other.

"No, that's my daddy!" Keeah exclaimed, running to the man and giving him a hug. She twirled around. "Meet my father — King Zello!"

The king smiled a huge grin. "Khan found me. Galen and Max are here, too."

The old wizard stepped from the shadows. He was dressed in long blue robes. "I am pleased that you children are safe." He looked at the Neals. "All of you!"

Galen's spidery helper, Max, clambered along the wall to them. "The magic stairs have appeared in the Kalahar Valley. We must hurry."

Just then, the air around them became all wavy. The stones in the square seemed to wiggle and turn clear.

Max scrambled in a circle around the children. "It's happening!" he chittered nervously. "The flying city of Ro — is disappearing!"

King Zello hoisted his wooden clubs, one in each hand. "You kids get to the ship.

Galen and I will distract the Ninns. Yee-haw!"

The Ninns turned from the ship. They grunted. They charged across the square.

Eric looked at his friends. "Everyone to Sparr's ship! Now!"

The four friends ran for the cargo door.

They leaped in.

Clang! The giant door on Sparr's airship slammed shut behind them.

Nine

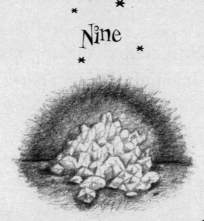

Mountains of Diamonds!

They jumped to their feet and looked around.

"Holy cow!" Julie muttered.

All around them were piles, mounds, mountains of shimmering, glittering diamonds.

"With these Sparr could make his whole Ninn army invisible," Keeah said.

"He'd be unstoppable!" Neal exclaimed.

"That's why we have to stop him now," said Eric.

One Neal started shaking his head. "I don't like being locked in Sparr's personal ship. A few hours ago, we were trying to get out of here!"

"Yeah, shouldn't we try to keep the ship from flying away?" the other Neal asked.

Suddenly, the walls rumbled around them.

"We're taking off," Keeah said.

"I have an idea!" the first Neal said. He entered a corridor of the ship.

"Where are you going?" the second asked.

No answer.

"Man, he never listens!" Neal grumbled.

Then, just as in the Tower of Memory,

Eric sensed that they were not alone. He turned.

"Looking for me?" said a voice.

Lord Sparr stepped into the cargo bay.

Slowly, Eric made his way toward him. The fins behind Sparr's ears went from purple to black. His face was full of anger.

"Princess Keeah," he said. "Say good-bye to your beloved world. I have read the future. Droon shall soon be mine!" He raised his hand to her. Red light leaked from his fingertips.

Keeah tried to jump away, but she slipped on the floor. Without thinking, Eric leaped in front of her.

"Watch out!" Neal cried out, jumping in front of both of them.

At the same moment, the other Neal raced in. "What? Old fish fins hurting my friends? As if!"

And he jumped in front of the other Neal.

Sparr shot a blast at them all.

Zzzz! Poomf! The air went red.

Eric pushed Keeah out of the way at the same time as both Neals crashed into each other.

Sparr bolted away into the depths of the ship.

"I'll get you!" yelled Eric. In a flash, he was on his feet and down a corridor after the sorcerer. He chased Sparr into the main control cabin.

Eric screeched to a stop. Cold air was rushing into the cabin. Sparr stood near an open hatch.

"Stay where you are!" The sorcerer's eyes burned with rage. But he did not try to hurt Eric.

"You're keeping me alive, aren't you?" Eric said. "Why? For what? Tell me!"

Sparr grinned. "Because of what will happen. Because of how you will . . . help me!"

"What?" Eric cried. "I'll never help you!"

"Time . . . will tell!" the sorcerer said. Then he lifted his cloak behind him and leaped from the hatch.

Eric crawled to the opening in time to see Sparr spread his cloak and swoop to the ground.

"I'll never help you!" Eric yelled to the wind.

When he ran back to the cargo bay, everyone was shaking their heads.

"Oh, man!" Neal groaned. "This is the worst!"

"Neal?" Eric said. "Where's the other you?"

"When Sparr blasted us we came together," he said. "Poof! There's only me now. I'm normal."

Eric jumped up. "Yahoo! Just you? You're just you! This is terrific! Boy, are we happy!"

Neal frowned. "We would be except for . . ."

"Except for what?" Eric asked.

"Except for what he told me . . ."

"What who told you?"

"The other Neal. Right before *we* became *me*."

"What did he tell you?" Eric cried.

"That he did something to the ship —"

KA-BOOOOM! The walls shook with a tremendous blast, throwing the kids to the floor. Flames leaped up the outside of the ship. Smoke began to fill the cargo bay.

"That!" Neal yelled, grasping for something to hold onto. "The other Neal did *that*! So Sparr wouldn't get away."

"But his plan sort of backfired," Julie said.

The ship rocked again, then started to dip.

"Uh-oh," Eric said, "I think we're going down."

"We are definitely going down," said Keeah.

Neal frowned. "Splat, anyone?"

Ten

The Sorcerer's Power

The nose of Sparr's giant silver airship tipped forward sharply.

"We're going to crash!" cried Neal.

"We're not going to crash," said Eric. "Sparr could have hurt us but he didn't. He read the future in the Tower of Memory and he let us live. We'll get out of this somehow. I promise."

The ship dived even faster.

"Um . . . how?" Julie asked.

Vrrr! Vrrr! Outside the cargo bay windows a small purple wingship pulled up.

"Daddy and Khan and Max and Galen!" Keeah shouted. "They followed us!"

Eric grinned. "Told you we'd be okay."

Julie clambered over the mounds of diamonds and hit a button on the wall.

Whoosh! A door opened.

"The tossing platform!" she said.

They all climbed out. The Droon night was deep blue. Flames licked up the sides of the big ship as Khan pulled his small purple ship closer.

"It's now or never, folks!" Neal said.

Clutching one another's hands tightly, the four friends jumped from the flaming platform. They landed right in the cockpit of Khan's wingship.

"Now you are safe!" King Zello said, hugging his daughter tightly to him.

Vrrr! Khan roared up and away as the giant flaming hulk dived to the earth.

In the sky nearby, the last traces of Ro were fading. The tall, lizard-like people of the city were gathered in the square to wave at the purple ship.

"Good-bye, Guardians," Neal said. "Good-bye people of Ro. Thank you!"

Suddenly — *ka-whoom!* — Sparr's silver airship slammed into a snow-covered mountain. It exploded with a tremendous fiery blast. A cloud of black smoke rose from the wreckage.

At that instant, too, a white light shone down from the fading city. The light rippled once and diamonds — millions of diamonds — flowed up from Sparr's burning ship.

"They did it!" Julie gasped. "They got the diamonds!"

A moment later, Ro drifted into the glowing white moonlight and vanished.

"Hey, I almost forgot!" Eric said. "When Sparr was in the Tower of Memory, he read something at the very top. Then he said the word 'ice.'"

Galen frowned. "Some new evil that Sparr is planning against our world. You have done well, Eric. You have all done well. Time will tell what this clue means. But one thing is certain. Sparr's power is growing. Be watchful, be careful. . . ."

"Look! Look!" Max chirped from the backseat. "The rainbow-colored stairs are ahead!"

Khan swooped the ship into the Kalahar Valley. He pulled up to the shimmering staircase.

Eric, Julie, and Neal climbed out and onto the bottom step. They turned to Keeah.

"We'll be back," Eric told her. "Definitely."

Keeah looked into their eyes. "Droon is lucky to have friends like you. I am lucky to have such friends."

"Any day," said Neal. "Anytime."

"Anywhere the stairs lead us," Julie added.

Keeah smiled. "The magic is with us all!"

The kids waved good-bye as Khan's purple wingship circled the rainbow stairs and flew up into the clouds.

The three friends ran up the steps and into the small room at the top. Then they turned once more to the midnight sky of Droon.

The fierce wind had died down.

Droon was at peace for a little while.

At least it seemed so.

Eric flicked the light switch on the wall.

Whoosh! The magic stairs vanished, and the gray cement floor was beneath them again.

Neal opened the door and they stepped out into the basement. The clock on the workbench had hardly moved at all. They had been gone only a few minutes.

"It seems like we've been in Droon for years," Eric said. He glanced back at the small door under the basement steps.

"I'm really tired," Neal said, yawning. "But I can't wait to go back. You might even say I'm *itching* to go back!"

Julie chuckled. "Me, too. I hope it will be soon. Maybe we'll actually stop Sparr. Maybe we'll help Keeah find her mother. That would be so cool!"

"Maybe," said Eric as they headed upstairs to the kitchen. Then he remembered Galen's words.

Be watchful, be careful. . . .

Eric shivered when he thought of all the bad things that might happen.

He felt cold somehow.

As cold as . . . ice.

ABOUT THE AUTHOR

Tony Abbott is the author of more than two dozen funny novels for young readers, including the popular *Danger Guys* books and *The Weird Zone* series. Since childhood he has been drawn to stories that challenge the imagination, and, like Eric, Julie, and Neal, he often dreamed of finding doors that open to other worlds. Now that he is older — though not quite as old as Galen Longbeard — he believes he may have found some of those doors. They are called books. Tony Abbott was born in Ohio and now lives with his wife and two daughters in Connecticut.

THE SECRETS OF DROON

A New Series by Tony Abbott

$2.99 each!

Under the stairs, a magical world awaits you!

❏ BDK0-590-10839-5 #1: The Hidden Stairs and the Magic Carpet

❏ BDK0-590-10841-7 #2: Journey to the Volcano Palace

❏ BDK0-590-10840-9 #3: The Mysterious Island

❏ BDK0-590-10842-5 #4: City in the Clouds